Briar Rose

And other Fairy Tales darkly Revisited

Alyxandra Harvey

Manor House

Briar Rose

Library and Archives Canada Cataloguing in Publication

Harvey, Alyxandra
    Briar Rose : and other fairy tales darkly revisited / Alyxandra Harvey.

   ISBN: 978-1-897453-81-0

   1. Fairy tales--Adaptations. I. Title.

PS8615.A7575B75 2011   C813'.6
C2011-907691-8

Copyright 2011-08-30 by Alexandra Harvey
Published November 28, 2011
Manor House Publishing Inc.
(905) 648-2193 www.manor-house.biz

First Edition. 144 pages. All rights reserved.
Cover design: Michael Davie/Donovan Davie

Special thanks to Jessica Kelly for the use of her captivating front cover photograph "Rapunzel"
To learn more about Jessica Kelly and her Work:
email her at crazyrandomhappenings@gmail.com
Web: http://www.facebook.com/CrazyHappenstance

Printed in Canada.

We acknowledge the financial support of the Government of Canada through the Canada Book Fund for our publishing activities.

Briar Rose is a work of fiction. All content is owed in its entirety to the imagination of the author. Any and all characters and situations are solely the creation of the author. Any perceived resemblance to real people/events in the pages of this book is purely unintentional.

Part 1
Briar Rose

Briar Rose

Author's Note:

Fairy tales didn't begin as children's stories. They were originally oral folktales thought to belong to the "peasant" class, until the literary salons of the 17th century adopted them as their own.
They have been retold countless times and hundreds of years later they still resonate. They are a guide through the dark woods of life and a conversation with our mythic selves.
Take another look.
The witch, the wolf and the wonder await.

Briar Rose

First Passage…

(i)

Let us say this story begins

one night in a castle,

though it could start anywhere, anytime.

Some details though are surely necessary.

There is a king then, and, as expected, a queen.

Say he is wise, and fond of mince-meat pies

and sharp cheeses at the end of a meal.

Say she is beautiful, only because we must,

but measure beauty by the way

she can part fighting dogs with a glance

or by the quickness of her fingers,

not for cross-stitch,

but rather for the kind of stitches

which leave scars.

everyone has a tale to tell of sickness or wounds

that

bleed too long,

or babes refusing to be born.
Still, this is not the beauty we are accustomed to —
it hardly seems a proper telling without the mention
of skin like pearls,
or emeralds and diamonds woven into hair bright as
summer wheat,
dark as winter sky.
Say all these things then,
and more.
It is enough at the moment that there is a queen,
that she has not died or turned cruel or has a womb
dry as salt.
Most of these stories do not have a true queen:
mothers are frail in this place.
One wonders what they are all escaping,
running from or running to.
Already, the castle is a castle,
well-built, decorated with lanterns and pomegranate
trees and tapestries of unicorns and odd flowers —
but still a building of grey stone, cold and damp as a
frog's home
but without the gentle lick of petals constantly
filling the edges of the water.
Here there is the beauty of the stars above,

yes,

and of torches burning and the scent of rosemary

and

mint from the garden.

But there is also the sound of swords sharpening on stone

and the creak of armour like bare branches on the

shortest day of the year

when the ice and the blue frost

are the only flowers worth picking.

This is not meant to be sinister, merely comforting,

common even.

(ii)

Hundreds of people sleep between these walls

and dreams gather in the corners,

thin as cobwebs,

clever as spiders.

On a night such as this one, old and sacred to some,

the moon hung heavy as honey between the long

and

lovely hands of the trees.

The wind was a whisper

and in the hall below the royal chamber, women are

singing.

It is the first of summer and there is dancing

in the fields

and ribbons

red

as

blood,

white

as

milk.

There are rumours, of course, of antlered men and

white deer women

and fires burning sweet until morning.

In the new year, when the snows come,

there will be babies crying across the countryside.

There is singing now, and feasting —

apples pressed into wine, soft cheeses, pears

ripening, berries slipping between eager lips.

There is darkness and also earth and sky.

Even in the castle, the feasting and the song.

It will be no surprise to you if I say a girl was

conceived on that wild night

when all the doors in all the houses and all the gates

in all the gardens

swung open.

There has been years of wishing and praying and virgin

finger-bones kissed for luck —

such irony when there is no time for irony.

Pilgrimages have been made to wells of healing water,

dressed with golden crosses

but older, far older than that.

The queen has been to each, bringing offerings of

incense and oranges and beeswax

and tiny babies carved in silver, naked as stars.

Lately she has been going barefoot in a white chemise

and

she has given her golden combs and silk slippers to the poor,

who have no use for such things.

But this night, as the sun reclines in a bed of lilac and peach,

the queen goes into the woods where the fairies make

merry

and where the old gods still walk between the trees

and the shining rivers.
She wears red and feels her breasts grow heavy.
She goes alone, as such things are done, and brings
gifts of honeycomb and cardamom seeds.
The old woman waits in a cottage under a strand of
willow trees with slender leaves
as bright as the May queen's hair.
She was crowned once, Old Mab, when the moon still
pulled the blood from her body.
She has worn the red roses and the white
and has
watched the young men
watching her.
Those same roses are brittle now,
hanging from the wooden beams,
tied with silver ribbons.
It is a place the dust will not visit, or the spiders
who know the mysteries better than we.
The fire in the grate sends sparks up the chimney,
exploding over the thatched roof like
giddy fireflies.
Old Mab waits and spins wool, the wheel creaking,
creaking

and her foot beating a pattern like the drums

in the woods,

in the hearts of stag and wolf

and white horse

and lovers in the dark;

the hearts of tiny

sparrow and bee and toad.

(They say three sisters live in a cave not far from

here and spin the wheel of fate, weaving the thread,

measuring the thread, cutting the thread.)

I know why you have come,

she says.

There are charms for such as you, if you would
take them from an old woman on a night such
as this one.

The queen thinks of priests and red wine and blue

cloaks.

The wheel continues its turning, like the sun, the

moon, the bleeding;

wood pedals clacking like a hundred insects,

beetles and blackflies and wasps,

like rain and seedpod,

like thunder and wagon wheel and fiery anvil,

spinning,

spinning

and her body a red rose on the vine,

tender bud opening, petal by petal, slow as love,

quick as

love,

the bee the pollen and those petals,

dropping

like blood and then

the white rose, the milk, the stars

and the moon swelling in her belly.

All this in a single breath in the old woman's

cottage

in the heart of the greenwood

where no one goes, uninvited.

Somewhere in the gathering darkness on the other

side

of the window,

something screams,

a rabbit or a mouse, a small creature anyway,

swelling the belly of an owl,

hungry and fierce.

The price you pay,

Old Mab says,

is to stand tall and not to forget

and not to deny me should you see me
at well, road or table.
The queen is sure she can feel a child growing
inside
her already.
She remembers tales of other queens, barren,
abandoned
under hazel-tree, broken mirrors, hearth-fire.
In this place, queens do not last, whatever their
beauty,
kindness
or wit.
Daughters are alone and men gather in halls and
councils to barter children
for chests of gold and the peace of a neighbouring
kingdom.
There is nothing so precious as a son to rule and a
daughter to sell.
This is the only world she knows.
She hasn't the courage to see the fires burning on
the
hills and the dancers shedding clothes like
petals,
leaves,

pollen.
She returns to the castle with a charm of red clover,
petals from a May Queen's
crown and a tonic of unicorn root in a glass bottle
the colour of blackberries bursting.
She craves raspberries, apples and black plums.
That night, the king is especially handsome
and the queen smells of roses.

(iii)
It is January
and the hills are heavy with snow
like pale lilies, yarrow and mayweed.
The ice is a crown on every tree
and the river is not speaking today.
This is the season of furs and fires
and babes born to the greenwood.
In the castle,
the queen has been the moon in the sky
for too long now —
certain promises must be kept.
Blood again,
but this time,
welcome.

Briar Rose

A story is being born and outside,

the trees are shaking,

the birds are gathering on the walls

and the owl is sleeping peacefully.

The room is full of light and women and roses,

hundreds sent from a king of a warmer country

who has a daughter,

mute and pretty as an orchid

and, just in case,

several unmarried sons.

Winter is delicate.

The screams of a woman in childbirth

are not.

There is more blood, and there is pain,

of course there is pain,

but soon, soon, there is also

a daughter.

A son would have been better.

Already the advisors are muttering

of princelings, boys yet to be born and the

marriage bed.

The girl is born on a blanket of fur

and white roses and

in every village

and every town and

every city, the wheels are turning

on wagons and toy horse and in

witch's cottage.

The wheels spin until morning, untouched.

(iv)

The moon is full

and everything is pale

under her clever fingers:

the valleys under the snow, the river, the ice,

winter everywhere hard and cold to show you

your every precious breath.

The white horses

are wild in the stables.

The doves have been coming for days now

and the crows,

and a single moth in the stone stair,

spiralling and not as lost as you might think.

The queen wears a gown sewn with diamonds and

pearls.

Moonstones are too common.

There is a young seamstress who will dance tonight,

fingers bleeding.

The king wears gold and is looking powerful

and pious.

In the chapel, the priests sing hymns

and give thanks.

The young girls are wearing blue cloaks

in honour of the Virgin.

There are candles everywhere and you would

be forgiven for thinking

you were feasting between the stars

and falling for the wishing.

Kings have come from far and wide

and queens and packs of royal children,

polite as watercress sandwiches.

Gifts have been brought:

hibiscus wine, papaya, red birds, pedants in the

shape of dragonflies,

bells to keep the devil away, pouches of saffron and

cloves,

butterflies in glass domes and

for the girl,

roses,

roses enough to fill her every glance and white as

milk;

Briar Rose

dried and dusted with gold, carved from willow and ash,
dipped in silver, sewn out of puckered satin, embroidered,
painted on tiny stones pulled from the Dead Sea,
oil in ivory bottles, roses pressed into beads and strung into rosaries,
thorns to be placed under the bed for protection
and a single blanket of woven roses, soft as water,
wild as a thunderstorm.
For music: the harp and the flute--
the painted drum is forbidden here,
banished to the forest, too earthy,
and dangerous
for corsets, narrow shoes
and carefully constructed dignity.
Still, on the other side of the moat filled with lilies,
in the woods
where there is dancing and fire,
a drum sounds.
Like horses running, storms breaking,
the mother of the earth herself breathing summer
and winter
and everything else in between.

The priests,
kind, and concerned,
ring the bells.
Still, the drum in the rivers of the blood,
under the skin, in the pulse in fingertips
and thigh, in the delicate
cage of corset bones.
The queen has already forgotten
the woods, the woman, and the wheel.
The table is set with seven gold plates
and seven gold spoons
and seven gold cups.
Seven queens have come with seven blessings for
the child:

The First:
The first, of course, is the wish
that she might be the most
beautiful
woman in the land,
which anyone can tell you,
is not a blessing at all,
unless we are talking of the kind
of beauty that creates or heals

or means something –

and we are not.

Better if she had offered

the old Navaho prayer: *may you walk in beauty*

which is a different thing altogether.

Even Keats knew it: *beauty is truth*

truth, beauty.

But here instead:

a small waist, long shining hair, soft skin

and a gift for silence.

The Second:

Wit.

Already, this is better.

We can hope for the wit of a woman

who knows her own mind,

of foxes and blackbirds and caterpillars,

of wild laughter

and a certain kind of honesty.

Instead:

diction and conversation which is not conversation

at all

though entertaining

and trained to carefully avoid

politics and religion.

Wit enough to amuse others,

especially princes,

and at your own expense.

The Third:

The Dance.

This is a gift, certainly, but not

the dance of bluebells under rain,

the dance of bellies and silver coins,

of painted bodies under a wanton sky

which will not hide for any reason.

This is not the speech of instinct,

the poetry of bones and bare feet,

the holler of a woman when the moon is full

and her thighs are on fire with love of herself.

Instead:

The pretty waltz, the carole and the pavan.

All lovely, and all

requiring a partner

who will lead you.

The Fourth:

Song.

To sing like the wren, starling or chickadee,

lifting your throat,

a pretty pursuit to benefit everyone.

A soft song though, smooth as peaches,

mild as cream.

No pepper, no lemons,

simply:

sugar.

Not a detriment necessarily,

but not a true blessing either.

The Fifth:

Music.

To play, which is not the same

as singing or dancing but rather

a marriage of the two.

This will teach compromise,

the importance of

the pause

between words

and the art of keeping the one you love

amused.

(Some songs are clearly forbidden:

those with thorns and spiders,

those with revolution or conjecture

and those you write yourself).

The Sixth:

Grace.

Slender wrists, a way of walking.

To be delicate and precious,

compared to pearls and silk,

and, of course,

gold.

The Seventh:

The seventh blessing is the meat of it:

a curse, a trick

or a choice.

(v)

The old woman enters the hall

and the spiders come

and the crows and a single red bird,

more beautiful than anything,

than poppy or candle or kiss.

Briar Rose

The music falters and the singing,

but not the drums faint as lightning,

pouncing like a cat in tall grass,

or the fires burning between the black trees.

The queen remembered a crown of roses,

red and white,

and the night she poured magic into her bed.

The priests cross themselves and kneel

on the hard stones

and one of the seven, a sister in a black habit,

slips behind a tapestry of St. George

slaying the dragon

and wonders if the Virgin burned like Old Mab in

her roses

and her cloak painted with wheat and red deer.

The men stand and reach for weapons

but the swords remember their first home,

still as a sacred lake.

The hounds expose their bellies.

Moths float out of the fires, like ash and snow.

The plates fill themselves with food:

oatcakes, honey and apple.

The bones in her hair clatter like ice

and seeds

and the snapping of branches in winter.
I've come with a blessing.
she says and pollen covers their hands
and roses bloom in the gilded crib.
The queen looks at the king
and the pale priests
and the whispering guests.
There is no room at the table.
Old Mab, denied, still speaks.
The child requires a true blessing:
That when the moon makes a woman of her
I will return and offer her the wheel, the spindle
and the blood.
A death in certain eyes, a life in others.
A true gift then: a choice.
The nun touches the tapestry and thinks of saints
beheaded and boiled and burned
and that too many choices lead to too many sins
and princesses cannot afford to want
what they cannot have
and she offers her own blessing, not yet spoken.
A long sleep, not a death, should such a choice be
offered
and the ability to forget. And, to make it sweet,

the kiss of a handsome prince.
There is silence for a moment
and then a royal decree:
no spinning wheels in this kingdom,
no chance, no choice.
Fool,
Old Mab is naked as crow wing, bear claw
and pale mushroom.
There are many kinds of sleeping.

(vi)
This is a story the girl knows well,
too well.
It is already difficult enough
to create your own myth and follow it.
Still, she knows certain things:
that princes rarely look like their portraits,
that songbirds sing best out of the cage
and that the forest is wide and full of secrets.
In her bed, when the castle sleeps,
and the cattle in the fields,
she listens to the drumming
and wishes she were a moth, a butterfly, a
dragonfly,

Briar Rose

anything with wings.

When she was little she would race through the halls

sticky with sugar and mud

and hard green apples stolen from the orchard.

Now she must walk

like a shaft of sunlight, steps small as berries,

small as dust motes.

She must wear white,

which shows all manner of dirt and indiscretions.

She wants the woods, the rivers and the fields.

She wants something she does not understand,

something she thinks she may have seen once;

a painted antlered man

waiting between the oak and the ash

and a woman, herself,

under the thorn tree and the moon.

Mostly, the man and the white stag

when the leaves are thick

and fill the air like rain.

She wants lightning and bluebell and grapevine.

Something is happening.

This much she knows.

Briar Rose

(vii)

In the morning,

her father calls her to the throne,

smiling, big hands full of presents

and candied roses.

She would rather eat wild mint leaves.

There is a certain smile she does not trust.

It is too much a meal of strawberries and cream

and caramel pudding,

and one she has had to wear too often

when she would prefer a supper of moth wings

and bee stings.

She is aware of a prince: familiar, waiting.

He is pleasant enough this one,

has not weighed the jewels in her hair

or cornered her when the candles go out.

Still, she is tired of growing live ivy

trained to circle the windowpane,

never allowed to reach outside

and go wild.

She wants to be a red bird falling out of that

window,

or a stone.

She wants to be anything but this.

Briar Rose

(vii)

The blood comes later,

burning between her legs

and making her aware for the first time,

that there is a moon waxing and waning

inside her body.

This is shouted as a good omen,

the princess is fertile

and betrothed.

But there are some women, she has heard whisper,

who take off their gowns

and slip into cool rivers

and drink wine and paint themselves

with pollen

at such a time.

In the castle, this is not done.

She must return to her chamber

and remain there for three days;

not to sing or dance or rest,

but to hide.

The body of a woman knows

the secrets of water and thunder

and of the earth turning to mud and glass

and of seeds, of course,

seeds breaking every manner of cage and cover.

She would be hyacinth, harebell, holly berry.

She hears the drums again,

nearer this time,

as if her heart were painted and stretched

under another's hand.

(ix)

At the top of the tower,

an old woman waits.

The girls finds her way,

follows the pulse of her own blood.

In this room, everything is

different.

The forbidden wheel turns slowly

and she wants to touch it,

wants to feel the warm wood,

the wool

and the sliver of silver as it slides under skin.

She has heard it told many times:

that a choice was offered to her though never

explained.

What will happen?

She asks,

Briar Rose

Will I lay down like the bear,
like a stag full of arrows,
like mushrooms when they are done being
mushrooms?
> *All things return,*
> *Cinderella only wanted poetry*
> *and Snow White solitude.*
> *They chose too late,*
> *or did not choose at all.*

Old Mab spins and spins and spins.
> *All things return.*
> *You will sleep or you will wake.*
> *Which are you doing now?*

(x)
She thinks of the marriage feast going on without
her,
of the marriage bed and
the forest, dark and sweet as a lover's mouth,
full of choices and promises.
She could turn away and there will certainly
be babies and bartering;
beauty and wit and grace
because others have told her so.

Briar Rose

She thinks of the fox every winter

hunting in the hills

and the mice in the pantry,

so full they forget to run from the kitchen cat.

When the wheel stops,

it is because her hand is upon it

and the thread twists and knots.

The needle is pale as antler,

as bone and tooth.

It is firefly and wasp

and quick as lilac in the spring.

Blood drips, a faint drum.

In the gardens, the roses are thick as clouds.

They spread like spilled wine, spilled blood,

crimson as sunset and sunrise.

They are everywhere, like fire.

She wonders if she will dream,

or die.

Old Mab smiles.

There are many kinds of sleeping.

Second Passage...

(i)

You find yourself in the forest,

where the lilies grow tall as towers

and there is rain and stars and eyes everywhere.

You want to touch everything.

Under your feet, pine needles,

soft and old as the sun

and the turtles living in the pond.

There are eggs buried under the sand there,

even when such things are impossible,

and swans gliding like noisy ghosts.

In the castle, the dogs are howling.

Here the earth is more beautiful

than tame tigers and tapestries

and rose-water fountains,

even when it turns to mud in your hands.

You rub it on your face

and over your white dress

and white pearls and white roses.

There are flowers here you have never seen.

You wonder what they might taste like,

and if they have a name

because surely everything here has a name.
You are aware that here are the answers
to everything,
pouring out of the sky and
the autumn leaves, the rivers and
the ash struck by lightning last year and
smouldering still
if only you knew the questions to ask —
which to speak out loud
and which to pose only in the pond and parks
of your own body.
You could walk for days,
whisper to the salmon and the hazelnut,
to the badger and the lynx and the starling.
Each would mention the poem of the wind,
the way the trees bend
but each would have a story
different than the rest,
sharp and heavy with its own beauty.
There is death here, of course,
the fear of the hunter and the dogs
but also bodies breaking open in the night,
some in hunger,
some in pleasure

Briar Rose

and never a moment a wasted.
There are some who have died already
and do not know it.
Here in the woods there are crossroads
everywhere.
If you wait too long
and will not choose a way—
this is another kind of dying
or sleeping.
Watching for signs is good
(following them is better):
a yellow leaf,
a certain kind of rain,
toad,
all leading somewhere.
Even walking blind
is sometimes better than standing
still for too long.
Only the heron has the trick of it
but he has wings which will take him
anywhere.
When a red bird lands in the birch tree
and watches you as if you belonged here,
he is the one to follow.

Briar Rose

It does not matter if you are afraid.

It does not matter if the brambles

and the vines conspire against you.

Follow.

Such a gift may not be given again

and never in the same way.

When you are lost

and think you have come back to where you began

— this is good.

But do not be fooled.

You are somewhere else entirely.

There are other girls who

have come this way—

some have left bells and henna

to mark their passage, to comfort you.

Others have left their bones,

licked clean by all the beasts of the forest.

Not every story is pretty.

The most you can hope for sometimes

is a choice.

Never mind.

Every story is beautiful.

That is the sort of thing

which makes a difference in the end:

the beauty you bring

and

how awake you are

when it is returned to you.

 (ii)

Notice the arch of the oak,

the acorns

and the torn leaves

and notice

the red bird breaking through

the branches

like the sun

or a ripe strawberry falling from the stem.

You are on the hills

and everywhere

the red-backed deer pause,

lift their heads,

eyes wide as lakes

when it is too dark to see.

You smell musk and fruit and

your own blood.

Someone is making a sound like a sigh

and you realize it is you.

You sit quietly, watching.

Briar Rose

It is surely a test of your
patience,
your courage,
and how aware you are of every blessed thing.
Time passes,
or it doesn't.
It hardly matters.
Perhaps the moon has come and gone,
perhaps the sun has stayed in the exact same
bed of sky.
The point is you are still here,
still open as a trumpet flower.
This is surely worth every fear
you ever had
and possibly more.
You are cold and still you remain,
This is prayer and poetry and
something darker
and even more beautiful.
And now,
just when you think you've become
grass, wildflower, insect—
one of them approaches you,
a fawn too young and too wise

to be afraid.

You are afraid

of your own breath

and would swallow it

if you thought it would keep her near.

She is all strength and muscle

and russet fur.

Her nose on your wrist is gentle, yes,

but persistent.

She will not leave this place without you

and the others are gathering in the twilight,

ready to run.

When you move you are hesitant,

stiff and wild-eyed.

It is the eyes they recognize first.

They let you walk among them,

a princess in a complicated gown and the red deer,

gathering, gathering.

moving over the hills like clouds,

following the wind or the moon,

some mystery you do not understand.

(iii)

You sleep curled against a warm flank,

sisters together,

all hoof and skin and delicate nostril.
You dream deer dreams of heather,
swimming in clear water and antlers.
As a girl you never dreamed
and this is enough to wake you briefly
and in waking,
you see stars and the breathing bodies
and the leaves shivering.
In the morning,
you run with them over the hills
warm with light and
between the trees,
which you rub with your bare hands.
Your dress is dirty now and you
find yourself on your hands and knees,
not humbled, but honouring
the raspberry vine, tasting the blueberry
and the late soft strawberry, nearly spent.
you drink from the river,
your reflection surprises you,
you half expect autumn fur, sensitive ears.
You want to grow hooves
and slap the earth like a drum.
You want the day to last forever.

Briar Rose

There is more running

and there is standing still,

but mostly,

there is running.

Your dress is torn now and tattered,

and you never noticed before the way

it wraps around your ankles

and that the corset is another kind of

prince or king or stepmother,

giving orders.

You want to wear the woods instead,

naked.

There are leaves in your hair instead of ivory

combs.

Your jewels are grapes, tiny plums, crab-apples.

The sun makes you all the russet and ochre of the

hind.

You know yourself in a way you never thought

possible —

instinctively.

You know without being told

that you would rather the mud over the masquerade,

that you do not like silk

and that the creatures of the woods,

all warm and wild,

understand you.

And finally, you know,

that there is always a choice —

choose spinning wheel, long sleep, marriage bed

or something else;

only choose,

do not wait to be

chosen.

You are running because you can-

this is not escape or fear, simply

love.

What you thought was a drumbeat

reveals itself as something much more than that

on a day such as this;

hooves on the ground

and the movement of deer in sacred places.

On the hilltop, the white stag

and in your hand, the warm tongue of hind,

urging you up – up.

(iv)

There are many kinds of crowns

and many kinds of kings.

This one you find by red bird and white stag

Briar Rose

and he wears antlers

and knows the secrets of the robin and the wren,

and the sun on water.

He has been waiting.

He is patient,

you are bare.

The fire burns and the stars

and the berries he will give you

when you are hungry.

He is amber and musk and wine.

You are apple already too long on the branch.

You feel yourself falling in this hands

and you swear there is only skin and night

and his mouth in all the worlds.

In the morning,

you are crowned with the white rose

and the red,

queen to his summer woods.

But you are alone.

A test, then – a test

Third Passage…

(i)

When I wake again,

Briar Rose

the sun is fierce as a mother bear.
They will tell me I slept no longer than usual
but it feels like a hundred years.
All that matters now is that my body
remembers who I am
and where I have been.
I crave long grasses
and remember the burning of a mouth on mine
though I can't be sure if that was dream
or waking.
The drums are louder now
and I see the shadow of antlers
on the wall
but when I lift my head I am alone
with the roses, the damned roses,
and the daylight sending a pattern
of tree branches on the stones.
There is sadness
but something else
too,
the knowledge that something has happened,
if only I could remember.
There is courage in the lifting of eyelids,

Briar Rose

like hummingbirds or trees daring to release every leaf
come autumn.
The light is like the heart of winter,
cold and breaking over everything.
They will talk about this day for years,
the day the princess wed
and the roses grew
and bled into everything,
even the snow.
They are gathered in the gardens,
in the stables, in every corner of the castle,
up the walls and scattered over the icy moat—
red as blood, red as berries, red as pomegranate,
cinnamon and watermelon,
red as the deer in the woods,
red as every wish I ever had for a lover,
a crown of leaves and the fires that burn in the hills.
Even my dress is red and velvet as new antlers.
No longer the white silk I have always hated,
the white silk which betrayed my every movement,
remembered every tree,
every muddy pause and pollen-soaked field.
I want to drink myself like wine.

Briar Rose

I am alone in the room with the spinning wheel,

the pale fleece turned crimson,

the drums sounding

And the shadows stroking me like fingers.

I could stand at the window all day.

Under the ice, the solstice is waking the berries in the woods,

the herons, the toads, the bats and the white stag who never sleeps.

(ii)

The hall is filled with candles and incense.

There will be a feast of roast duck and hazelnuts,

apple butter and almond cookies,

pomegranate stew and potatoes carved like roses.

The prince will be handsome.

He will smell like lemon soap and peppermint.

I prefer anise and wood smoke.

No one has asked me if I will miss the forest

when he takes me to his home,

or if I like the sound of his voice or the way

he touches my hand.

They have been preparing for this for months,

years,

and secretly they are pleased that I have slept

Briar Rose

too long today.

I am not surprised that my gown is already finished

and pale as the moon, as pearl and honey.

I have never seen it and it fits me perfectly.

It does not matter that I have said

I will not wear white again

or that all of the roses are red now.

There are traditions and the price has said he

likes me in white.

The sun is still shining.

There is more singing, I suspect,

to drown out the drums frantic in the forest,

which make the guests nervous

and pensive.

I am realizing that my heart

will not be silenced so easily—

more than a river, a plum pit,

more than watermelon seeds.

More than walnuts cracking or black grapes.

More, more, more.

I have wild ideas now,

of climbing out of the tower

on a rope

of red roses,

Briar Rose

of running the hills and

plucking my own petals.

I am unprepared for this,

and ripe for it, ripe enough

that the bees and the butterflies are waking

in their winter beds.

I imagine that under the trees,

the stag, the muskrat, the wolf

are all lifting their heads

and tasting the wind, watching the castle

and eating roses instead of the wild banquet

of each other.

I would join them if I could.

Already the fires are being lit

and a man crowned with antlers is painting

his body with spirals and waiting.

I must paint mine with perfume

and holy water.

I refuse to wear the white dress

and instead I wear burgundy velvet, and the roses,

of course,

though they are scarlet as a maiden's blush

and other parts.

Briar Rose

(iii)

The ceremony begins without us,

It is mostly about treaties and borders anyway.

It is the first time we have been alone,

the prince and I.

When he hands me a rose,

it is white as winter.

I think of the years I have spent in this place,

decorated with pale flowers like stars in water

when what I wanted most was the entire sky,

not kept in a pretty bottle,

but where it is meant to be,

wide and dangerous and exactly

everywhere.

I think of hours spent singing for princes

who were not listening and did not care

or else were as uncomfortable as I was.

I think of my hair,

neatly brushed and coiled and carefully curled,

dripping pearls.

My eyes demure and courteous because that is the

beauty I was blessed with,

the grace and the song.

How different might my story be if

Briar Rose

the seven blessings had been:
courage, creativity, a love of solitude,
strength, compassion, confidence and
the ability to be truly awake.
And must I wait for them to be given,
or can I create them for myself out of blood and
bone?
All that will change today will be the scenery.
Another palace, perhaps no roses, perhaps instead
gardens with monkeys and peacocks
and the unrelenting obedience of being a princess.
It is not this castle and its painted corners
which I will miss, but the view of the forest
outside my window
and what I might discover about myself there
if I had the chance,
or if I took it.
When I tell the prince I have a secret
perhaps we could find some other form of happiness
between the trees,
at first he wonders why I am not wearing
the white he is so fond of.
When he speaks it is only to say
You are nervous.

Briar Rose

and

It's perfectly natural.
But the castle is what I am used to
and what I have been promised—
they will measure our love
by how much gold the guests are given
and by the diamonds in your hair
and besides the forest is no place for a lady
and here is where we will stay
and you will learn to love it again.
I mention the singing of the robin in the morning,
the way the bear licks honey off her paw
and laughter.
You will learn to love it again,
he repeats and
A princess cannot be selfish in this way.
When the doors swing open,
the priests are there waiting
and my parents with rings of braided gold.
I think of all the princesses,
all the queens and all the stepmothers
who have stood where I am standing,
promised to a life, *chosen* because they did not
think to choose otherwise.

Briar Rose

I taste leaves in my mouth and musk

and sometimes it is the not knowing

which will kill you slowly,

sometimes it is the fear of choosing unwisely

and sometimes

none of it matters

but your own two feet

running against the earth

and a mystery

waiting

there.

Also,

a man who is not afraid,

but mostly

yourself

bare as the deer in the woods

where the drums are sounding,

because you are truly awake now

and because in the garden of your breast

your heart is bursting

like a red rose,

like a single red rose.

Go now – surely you are done with sleeping.

Part 2
The Rose Sisters

Briar Rose

Briar Rose

The Rose Sisters

i)

my sister and I lived in the forest

as all fairy tale princesses must,

though we were not princesses at all, but little wild creatures

who made a noble court of wren, fox and stag.

we held exquisite balls every summer evening,

and wore the stars like crowns and danced barefoot

until we grew tired as wilted lilies.

we slept in the green darkness with moss under our cheeks

and a river sword-bright at our feet.

in winter we sat by the fire and spun at the wheel,

the wood creaking like a ghost treading the floorboards.

mother would read to us and pour tea from a copper kettle.

autumn was my favourite, when the roses bloomed

plump as newborn babies.

Briar Rose

i was born there in the garden under the rosebushes
and mother named me
rose red
because she could not tell
petal from blood from baby.
my sister is pale as december
and winter is her friend, closer even
than me.
i used to wish i could be bright as fire and melt the
snow from the clouds.
mother named her
snow white
because she is cold and fragile and lovely as the thin
layer of ice
that sometimes makes a bed on the skin of the river.

ii)
mother was already an old woman when she had us,
or so she used to say.
the townsfolk called her crone and witch
but to us she was a queen who slept on pillows
filled with feathers.
i always preferred soft leaves and wild violets
and so did my sister until that winter.

Briar Rose

iii)

she began to crawl into the narrow bed and curl into the clean linens.
she left me dreaming in the ferns and i never knew i was alone
until i woke and felt cold.
we were close as roses
once.
i think she grew leggy and stretched the way some flowers do
when they grow too close.
i didn't want to be at her side in the small warm cottage
with the old rocking chair
but i didn't want to be left behind either.
i came in late at night or early in the mornings,
trailing a cloak of leaves and cold wind
and sometimes i told her stories of the wren-prince i would marry
or the stag that would carry me on its back
to the exact heart of the forest
where they say there is only silence.
i waited for some remark, a comment or a laugh--
anything to prove i was still alive.

Briar Rose

iv)

mother grew older and snow white grew thinner and pale

and seemed bright as the sword-bright river.

i was wild as a thorn tree,

and felt awkward in my skin,

as if it was some stolen magic cloak

that might turn on me at any moment.

there was warmth and the spinning wheel and the falling snow outside,

and for a moment it was like we were children again

and i could smell something dark and musky and forbidden

and suddenly

suddenly

a knock came at the door

which had been silent all our lives

(though in the winter we welcomed birds and wounded foxes and once

even a wolf who smiled prettily)

but no one had ever knocked before.

my sister grew demure as gladioli and i was still a fat peony.

Briar Rose

mother woke in her chair and bade us welcome the stranger,
winter's guest in a home of snow and roses
and fire.

v)
the man at the door might not have been a man at all.
he seemed to me to shuffle and amble and walk like a beast unused to his legs.
he wore a thick pelt of dark fur with a bear's head lowering over his own,
teeth and eyes gleaming.
his smile was as large as the rest of him, cloying as wet lilies,
dark as mud, wild as the bear he resembled.
he didn't speak and i began to wonder if he truly was a bear
but i did not like him
the way i liked the sleeping bears in the caves.
snow white offered him tea and honey and warm bread
and did not speak to me at all,
even when i burned my fingers on the kettle.

Briar Rose

she was fascinated by his dirty hands.
i might have hated her then.

vi)

he fell asleep by the fire and we sat up,
three women in the quiet woods
listening to his snores like thunder trapped in a jar
or ice breaking.
i longed to be outside in the storm,
but snow white watched him eagerly and gently, as
if he might wake
and see her there, kneeling in a gown the colour of a
cold moon
with her smooth hair and slender neck.
i feared the bear might eat her up, think her more
precious than honey.
i stayed awake all through the night and my eyes
grew heavy,
watching my sister watching a stranger.

vii)

morning was bright and hard as an eggshell.
the bear had already left and both my sister and i
fell asleep despite ourselves.

Briar Rose

snow white found a little hank of hair caught in the door
and she braided it and slipped it into her locket
when she thought i wasn't looking.
she found the heart of her forest and i could not even hear it beating.

viii)
i searched for long days for my own wren-prince or stag-king,
for someone who would be my white rose.
i searched at night when the moon was my candle,
and i found elm and thorn and ash and oak and ivy and nothing else,
no green embrace,
no enchanted frog
or casket of enchanted fairy gold turned to maple leaves.
once i thought i smelled something but i couldn't be sure,
and it was growing cold and i had been alone too long.

Briar Rose

ix)

you might think i should have been the one to be the bear maiden,
that my hard feet and clever fingers would have followed the beast,
but i was too near and too wild and already felt too beastly,
and it was snow white who had no darkness
and wanted it ferociously.
winter gave up after that.

x)

spring was abrupt and showy.
i counted rain puddles and rose buds
and snow white walked and walked and i followed.
she did not see me or the trees,
and only followed broken branches
which might lead her to her beloved.
i wondered if she still knew my name.
i snapped twigs under my bare feet and slapped at the leaves
while my beautiful silent sister wandered like the wind
between the birches.

Briar Rose

i lost my sister for the first time that day,
even though she was already gone.

xi)
my hair tangled and caught in the peeling bark of an old thorn tree
and i called out for snow white
but she was already following the sound of bees.
i yanked and ripped and tore but my hair was strong as chain,
and the tree seemed to grow arms like a lover's embrace,
only darker.
i used the knife at my belt, the one for berries and herbs,
and i cut through my stubborn hair.
when i finally got home mother was asleep
and snow white did not notice.
her hair was pale and reached her ankles.
her locket was a star swinging from her throat, thin as a sword between us.

xii)
the next day we walked again and i stayed close

and avoided the trees and when we stopped to drink from the river,
i drank from my own mouth and it was like falling through a mirror,
and it was almost enough,
even when snow white left
and there was only sky behind me.
it seemed easier somehow to fall into myself,
to let the cool soft hands of water hold me close as a sister.
i don't know how long i floated there with my eyes closed
and wet violets like gentle kisses on my mouth.
i only know that it was not snow white who pulled me out, but a thought:
> *this is not the centre*
> *this is not my heart.*

and that's something at least.
xiii)
on the third day, because there is always a third day,
snow white heard a branch breaking
or honey dripping
and rushed into the caves that opened like mouths
on the other side of the river.

i don't know what she saw there or how long she stayed.
i didn't watch her leave,
because there was sunlight suddenly burning into my eyes,
and then an eagle swooping down so low
it touched me with its wings.
i followed because that's what you do when you see an eagle,
and it was me who left this time, not her,
and it was me who ran wild as a hedgehog through the woods,
with a feather in my hair until the air seemed too perfect,
and the eagle passed over the sun again, and i was alone
and loved it fiercely.

xiv)
somewhere far away my sister dug her fingers
into a prince's shaman-thick fur.

Briar Rose

Part 3
Twelve Dancing Princesses

Briar Rose

Twelve Dancing Princesses

(first published online in "goblinfruit")

i)

you'll think we were giddy as birds in spring,

as buds opening on the willow tree like green kisses.

what else but love or wine,

would make twelve sisters run away when night is coldest,

and dance like we were putting out flames or crushing grapes,

dance until our shoes wore out and were as thin as we were.

ii)

you never met father.

he had hard angry hands,

Briar Rose

and mother never learned to dance or disappear.
she was a candle flame under his icy winter glare.
we danced because we were cold and there was nothing else to do.

iii)
it was our way of screaming,
though the bards and the storytellers
only saw satin slippers and the delicate arches of princess feet.
but even princesses blister when they dance from dusk to dawn.

iv)
when father unlocked our door in the morning,
to his twelve starlings all sleeping together, precious as pearls.
he was furious and confused: he had the only key
and yet our jeweled embroidered shoes were thin as paper.
it was the cost that enraged him and the not knowing.
our smiles did not help, and for that i'm grateful.

Briar Rose

he made speeches and proclamations
and had messengers ride to the edge of the kingdom
offering gold and other rewards for the man who
would solve this mystery.

v)

if he'd asked any of the women in the castle,
mother or the chambermaids, the servant girls, the laundresses,
they might have told him that we danced because
princesses can not run away,
that we danced because he would not let us speak,
that we danced to be closer to the moon, the forest, the rain;
that we snuck out of a secret door
painted behind one of the headboards.
they all knew the mystery, but no one gave us away
because father never thought to ask the women,
and because they longed to follow.

vi)

the first to arrive was the third son of a second prince

or a cousin to the high priest or just a knight wandering.

we only knew him as the first one,

the one father pushed into our rooms with that smile we all hated.

we never asked his name and he never asked ours.

he thought he would get twelve kisses and twelve babes in arms,

and he was wrong.

we gave him twelve smiles and a cup of spiced wine

and he thought it proper and encouraging and drank it down,

and sat in his chair,

 and crossed his ankles,

 and watched us carefully

until the wine began to work

 and he slept deeply

and dreamt of princesses dancing in tall grass and starlight.

vii)

when he woke we were already dressed in our favourite gowns

Briar Rose

watching him quietly, perched on the edge of our beds,
like hummingbirds.
he was still as a deer and suddenly we felt like wolves.
the key rattled in the lock like gilded bones,
that awful clatter that made us lean towards the hidden door
like a wheat field under a heavy wind.
we didn't know it then, but perhaps we should have guessed.
father said he acted like a king that day and
the first of our watchers died on the gallows,
swinging like a milkpod burst into the pale pale stuff of legends.
and we, the twelve, danced,
because we didn't know what else to do
and sometimes you die a little when you do nothing at all.

viii)
the next one told us he was a knight.
we were going to tie him up, knowing he would not drink the wine,

Briar Rose

but father would find him in the morning
and how would it look to be bested by twelve princesses,
and besides the storytellers would only leave that part out.
so we hit him over the head with a pot
and dragged him down the tunnel into the night
and left him in the forest with an unlit candle and a small fire
to keep the wolves away.
in the morning, father told everyone he'd had him killed,
had his head cleaved from his worthless body
and everyone believed him.
i still think about that knight sometimes.
i hope the wolves were kind and that he thinks of us sometimes too,
not as princesses or dancing girls,
 but as sisters who showed him the way out.
that is our most precious gift in this place.

ix)
it was the third prince and the third night
but you probably knew that already.

Briar Rose

father never did have any imagination.
even when he died, not long after,
he wasn't killed by
a falling tree or poisoned meat or a candle left
carelessly by his bed.
he died during dinner in the middle of a speech.
it was a lovely wedding gift and i'm sure my eldest
sister still remembers it fondly.
you'll think me hard, not a princess or a pale girl,
but someone with too many teeth.
i ought to suffer delicately, in velvet corsets with
star-lily eyes.
that's how it's always done in the old stories.

x)
we danced savagely and fiercely that night
and i'm not sorry for it.
if he hadn't locked us away every night,
we would have locked the door from the inside,
and we did sometimes because no one listens to
children
especially when they are beautiful.
so we danced,

and the last prince drank the wine even though he had heard the stories,
and the moon rose and poured in through the windows,
and it was full and ancient and called us out to the lake
where the swans slept and the forest folk still kept to the old ways.

xi)

it was in the tunnel that i first heard it,
a slight scrape, dirt loosening from the walls.
but no one listens to the youngest, not even her sisters.

xii)

they said it was a rat and i was just nervous and silly.
i followed, the last in a line of princesses walking through the damp,
following the tracks of our shoes from previous nights.

Briar Rose

i was the last to emerge into the cool wind off the lake,
and the moon burned above me and when i turned back,
i thought i saw a shadow, something darker in the dark
but then it was gone,
and there was only the lake and the others waiting in the boats,
the princes who were third sons or forgotten cousins
or had once been frogs, or wrens, or voices in the corridors.
the ones who escape—
we were the ones who danced, because we had to.
you'd never know it to see it,
but the little island crowded with pine trees
was more precious to us than palaces and crowns of gold.

xiii)
when the boats eased into the water i heard a faint splash,
an unnecessary sound,
but i knew what my sisters would say:

Briar Rose

it was a fish or a heron in the distance
and i let them speak louder than my bones,
 and the pale shiver which tickled my spine.
we danced savagely and fiercely that night,
and grew wings and crowns and fireflies for hair.
the clouds were like honey when we finally grew
too tired to circle the trees.
we had to run back along the hidden passageway,
stumbling, our toes and our heels pressing through
our shoes,
which gave away completely, like spider's webs.

xiv)
we were barefoot when we finally fell into our
perfectly made beds,
and we could hear father's footsteps starting to
move overhead
and in the stairwell and that's when we saw him,
the prince, leaning against the locked door.
the wine he had quietly spat back into its jeweled
goblet was dark
and seemed to watch us like an eye,
the cut on his forehead still bled.

Briar Rose

xv)

he bowed to us ,

and for a moment we could only look at one another

until the moment shattered when my eldest sister

stepped forward.

i wanted to shout

> *you were right*
>
> *it was a rat*
>
> *but not the kind you thought*

but even now no one would listen to the youngest,

and it didn't matter because the key slid into the

lock with its bonedance song

and the door swung open,

and father was there, large and red and furious,

and the prince only laughed and took my sister's

hand,

and said they would be married without dowries and

banns,

and father thought of the gold and the pearls

and the friendship of a neighbouring kingdom,

and he forgot about twelve daughters dancing a

wish under the moon

to be free of him.

Briar Rose

and in some stories the prince might have chosen me
because i was the youngest,
and i had been the one to hear him in the darkness
but in this story he chose the eldest because she knew
the
way
out.

Part 4

Little Red

And

To the Wolf

Briar Rose

Briar Rose

Little Red
(first published in Tesseracts 11, Edge Publishing)

(i)
You think you know this story.
you read it as a child
or discussed the meaning of the colour red,
and the metaphors of animal instinct
in university classes,
when you wore only black
and drank byron, tennyson and keats in smoky pubs,
at worn wooden tables, with girls
wearing eyeliner.
it isn't that kind of a story, not really.
oh, i wore red and lived in the forest
but my grandmother was a bitch,
and i never brought her warm cookies in covered baskets.
we never went to see her and it wasn't just because
the wolves and the winter were between us.

Briar Rose

ii)

i used to crawl out onto the roof at night when
everyone else was sleeping
to breathe the smoke from the hearth and lift my
white throat
and sing with the wolves and wild dogs
and all creatures who worship the moon.

iii)

i never had a red cape, satin or velvet;
we couldn't afford such things.
but my moon time came the first time i went into
the woods
after dark.
i felt powerful, sharp as the stars
with the blood between my legs.
this is what a woman does,
this is the true story of capes and crones and
handsome men
when the woods are full of silver eyes,
like pebbles in the river or rain when everything
else is
dry.
i never saw the handsome man,

Briar Rose

the woodcutter or the woodcutter's son,

who were said to speak the language of the beasts,

though i dreamt about them

every night.

that day i bled for the first time,

a red apple

was left on the step outside our front door.

i didn't know if it was the woodcutter's son

or the wolf.

i wasn't even sure there was a difference.

it was cold that day and i was barefoot,

running swift as a red deer between the silent trees.

i'm still not sure if i found them or if they found me.

iv)

they stood in a clearing of winter-bitten grass

with their breath white as frost from perfect nostrils,

flared, recognizing the scent of blood and wanting,

the scent of family.

sometimes the nobles from nearby towns hunt the wolves,

thinking only of thick pelts, black and silver,

to hang next to tapestries embroidered by pale-eyed women,

Briar Rose

or to lay at their feet and make them feel like kings.
i only wanted to know how it felt to be part of such a family
and never to fear winter or lightning.
the nobles always left the forest with broken bones and blood
under their nails and wild wild
eyes.

v)
i never really left.

vi)
i slept among them that night,
and bared my throat to the moon and licked the stars.
i dripped blood and never tried to see if their veins were warm
and if their blood ran blue and silver as the northern lights.

vii)
the oldest one died that night,

Briar Rose

a grizzled female with broken whiskers and
knowing eyes.
the wolves sang and howled and cried
and i wiped my blood over her paws that she might
run faster into the underworld.
the youngest carried a sharp edged rock
between tender teeth and dropped it at my feet.

viii)
they formed a circle around me, like mist around the
moon
or the stone circles in the south.
there was only their hot breath and mine and the
trees
whispering.

ix)
the youngest bit my hand when i tried to leave
and blood dripped onto the cold fur and the stone
was like a knife
or an icicle poised over your head
when there is wind in the forest.
the sharp edge slid between fur and flesh
and i peeled her like an apple.
there was blood in my mouth.

Briar Rose

you'll think this was harsh, brutal even
for a young girl only twelve,
and that such work should be left to men
with heavy arms or women with scars.
i can only say it was simple and warm
and i never considered making a muff or rugs to sell
at the market.

x)
instead
i slid into her skin, her body her breath,
and i was finally a woman and a beast and the forest
and i ran
and i lay down among the warm bodies
and dreamt of a girl in a house on the edge of the
woods,
still sleeping.

Briar Rose

To the Wolf

i)

they say that in the dark forest of night, all things make sense.
they say this especially when nothing makes sense.

ii)

please come back.
i have searched all the day and all the night long
and have found nothing but the mud of the swamp
where once there was a pond.
it was like this the first time i saw you.
do you remember?
you said: *don't run.*
i might have expected something more poetic.
it was spring after all,
and everything was as green as dandelion leaves,
so delicious after a long winter of salted meats and boiled roots
and the noxious fumes of tallow candles.
the frogs were singing their first song of the season.
the light had a citrus quality,

as if the sun was a fruit ready to be picked from the field of the sky:
a lemon maybe, or a clementine.
no wonder the frogs sang, even knowing there was more snow on the way.
there is always more snow on the way.
but in that moment there was only
the small green peeper in her soggy parlour,
shouldering the steep gradation of light through the bare branches.
and you.

iii)
in older stories than this one, there would be a witch in the woods
or icicles or breadcrumbs,
not a dainty speckled frog
who might sink into the mud and lily roots at any moment.
come to think of it, wolf or drowning, it's the same story.

iv)
 let's go back, just for a moment. a house, a song, sunlight.

Briar Rose

v)

it's no good. the wolf won't be ignored.

you were so beautiful with teeth like opals.

the air was grey as stone but soft,

something you might wear over your shoulders

when winter comes.

you see, the wolf is not the only danger in this story.

you had the blue eyes of a hunter,

hands laced with scars.

my grandmother warned me about men like you.

i thought i knew better.

sometimes, i still think so.

there was such a wildness to you, surely it was

worth it in the end.

you tasted like berries and smoke and i was

instantly drunk.

i can't imagine what you saw in me, just a village

girl

in a red cloak who liked the solitary business of the

forest best.

i never wore silk or velvet

and was more intimate with the sparrow and the

badger's den

than curtsies and porcelain tea cups.

vi) all the animals fled from you.
except for me.
i can still feel the weight of your hand on my hip.

vii) i stopped keeping rabbits as pets after that.

viii) the embers catch in the hearth.
a squirrel lands on the roof,
leaping from the pine trees as if she could improvise wings
if she has calculated badly.
i nearly believe her.
it is almost time to boil the water, bake the bread.
i lie under blankets that still smell like you,
listening in the red darkness
to the green song of the frogs
and i finally understand every word that is not being spoken.

ix) in the forest, yes.

Briar Rose

Part 5
Rapunzel revisited

Briar Rose

Briar Rose

Rapunzel revisited

First Part...

(i)

I will tell you the story

as it was told to me.

Before I was born, my mother

longed for rampion leaves

all through the long winter

when there was nothing to eat but

snow and ashes,

and the wrinkled turnips in the cellar.

every night she wept for want

of green leaves,

until she ate all the mint

in the medicine cabinet out of desperation,

and then the dried parsley

though it was bitter and stringy when boiled.

still, my mother's appetites would not be appeased,

and she blamed me for it,

and writhed and wept in her bed

until my father feared for us both.

He brought her pine needles to chew

Briar Rose

and made cedar into a weak tea

but still

she

wanted

rampion.

He cut the tops off the onions sprouting

in the winter baskets

but they were too bitter.

She wanted the roots mashed with vinegar

so he mashed the precious garlic bulbs in

the storeroom,

but still,

it was no use.

(ii)

On the last day of winter

or the first day of spring,

depending on who is telling the story,

my father peered over the stone wall

into Dame Gothel's garden.

The snow had melted away,

dripping from the eaves

through the mouths of gargoyles

to gather in the stone basins.

The tips of new grass

Briar Rose

poked up through the mud
and the birch trees
waved their yellow catkins.
By our front door,
the first crocus and hyacinth,
the wide mouths of tulips opening
and the pretty pale bonnets of daffodils,
like little girls clustered under the sun,
sharing secrets.
By Dame Gothel's back door:
poppies for sleep,
belladonna for secrets, and
apple seeds gathered in a bottle for
the husband who strays,
and, of course,
the first tender leaves of rampion.
Everyone knew her gardens
were the best in the kingdom.
Even the king brought his daughters
when they were ill
and Dame Gothel's teas and tinctures
always put them right again.
She still offers thyme for nightmares,
dill weed for stomach aches,

Briar Rose

and lungwort infusions for the winter cough.

She has shown me how to plant

the seeds when the moon is waxing,

to plant bulbs when it is waning,

and nothing at all

when the sky is dark.

It is better to dig into the earth

with a curved blade

of silver,

to leave a penny as a gift,

and to be naked

as the badger

in

her

den.

Even then she was respected as a healer

and a midwife,

with a gift for seeing into the

heart of things.

I tell you this because it is important.

(iii)

When she caught my father

sneaking over the wall to steal

Briar Rose

her rampion,

she could have had his

fingers

cut

off

at

the

joint.

(iv)
Everyone knows that to steal

from Dame Gothel

is to steal from the ill, from the infirm

and,

if that is not warning enough,

from the king's daughters.

On that first night,

she let the dogs loose in the

garden,

watching from the mullioned windows.

I can tell you exactly how she looked

though I was still floating inside

my mother's rampion-starved belly:

stern, wise

Briar Rose

and a little bit sad.
She has seen too much
and the lines on her face
are not easily read
by those who will not try.
It is not a coincidence
that some see only
an old witch with the
knowledge of poisons.
My father climbed back over the wall,
fingers already stained with mud,
though he had nothing in his pockets
to show for his trouble.
He took the last turnip from the cellar
and mashed it with the
last of the salt,
but mother dashed the plate against the wall
until it broke apart
and her fingers bled.

(v)
On the second night,
my father climbed over the wall again.
Dame Gothel waited for him.

Briar Rose

Your wife will not thank you,
she said, as gently as she knew how,
which,
it is to be admitted,
was probably not all that gentle.
If you take the rampion,
your child will be mine.
I don't know what my father heard,
if he even took the time to listen.
He slunk home like a chastised dog,
empty-handed once more,
and my mother wailed and gnashed her teeth
all through the night
until he thought blood would
come out of his ears,
until she choked on her own tears
and went white
as boiled mandrake root.

(vi)

On the third night,
there was no one to stop him.

Briar Rose

Iron bird cages sat over the rampion

and the strawberry,

to keep them safe from hungry birds

and rabbits

and thieves in the night,

but nothing would keep my father

away,

not that night.

He picked all of the rampion he could find,

and carried it back home

in his shirt,

cradling it like a baby bird.

(vii)

That night,

for the first time since the midwinter fires,

mother smiled at him

and was like the woman he had married,

back when they could drink snow

and eat turnips for all the cold days

and none of it mattered.

She ate the rampion,

tearing at it with her teeth,

sucking at the roots until they fell apart,

until her teeth were muddy,
until the hunger pains
were replaced with a different sort of pain
altogether,
one that nothing will stop,
not moon or old woman,
not even
love.

(viii)
I probably don't need to tell you
that my mother didn't survive.
The rampion soured her stomach
as it always did, making her ill,
even as she struggled
to free me from her body which was
breaking open under the stars.
When she died,
my father had her buried under stone,
where no green thing could grow.
He didn't know what to do
with more wailing,
even from his own child,
and so he left me

at Dame Gothel's back door,
under the bird cage
which had cradled the rampion.
He left on the next fishing boat
and lived on water,
where nothing green will grow,
for the rest of his days.
And Dame Gothel was right,
that night,
in the garden.
I became hers.

Second Part...

(i)
I loved living in the cottage
at the edge of the forest.
No one ever moved into my
parents' abandoned cottage,
people whispered of
bad luck
and hungry spirits.
Dame Gothel and I were mostly
alone

Briar Rose

except for the dogs she
kept for protection and
the folk who came to seek her
help.
Mostly they came for medicines
but sometimes,
at night,
they came for something else.
You could always tell
by the very first knock,
if they came for
other kinds of medicine,
the ones for luck
or love
or dreams of the future.
Those knocks always came
at the back door,
by the empty patch of earth
where rampion once grew.
I can remember lying in my bed
under the window,
with the quilt over my head
as Dame Gothel bustled in
front of the fire.

Briar Rose

In the morning,

she would teach me how to grind seeds

in the mortar and pestle,

how to braid stalks of hay to make

dolls for fertility,

and how to hang fleabane and lavender

to dry for sachets to

keep the bugs from our dresses.

I didn't learn to throw the bones

and read their patterns

or to lay out the tarot cards

she painted herself

under the full midsummer moon.

That summer she only taught me

when to pick the wild carrots, and

how to tell the poisonous mushrooms

from the ones that went

into the stew pot.

I ran in the woods

until my skin was dark as hazelnuts,

until my feet were hard as hooves,

and my legs quick as the red fox.

I loved every moment of it.

My father sent me seashells

Briar Rose

every year on my birthday
but aside from that it was just Dame Gothel
and I
and the gardens between the walls.

(ii)
I was weeding around the valerian
when I heard the sound of carriage wheels
and horse hooves.
I ran to the gates,
dirt under my nails and burrs in my hair,
to watch the pretty painted door swing open on
gold hinges.
I'd only ever seen anything half so pretty
made out of sugar and candied violets
the one time Dame Gothel
saved the baker's dog from losing a paw
to a hunter's trap.
The carriage had four outriders
armed with swords and lances
and the driver looked as if he could have
wrestled a bear
and still had breath left
to cool his porridge.

Briar Rose

The woman who exploded out of the door
shaped like a giant clam shell,
wore panniers under her striped skirts
which had been crushed en route
so that she looked oddly
deflated,
like a red cap mushroom
falling in on itself
in the deepest part of the forest.
I didn't recognize her
but she went straight to the front door.
She probably didn't even know
we had a back door.
A man in a silver frock coat
embroidered with peacocks carried
a flushed boy inside the cottage.
I snuck in the back
to listen as they discussed
his illness
and settled him onto a pile of
wolf furs by the fire.
> *We've had the red fever,*
> *so you can leave the boy here.*
Dame Gothel told them as I crouched

Briar Rose

behind the chest of clothes.

I knew she knew

I was there,

there was never any hiding

from Dame Gothel.

Even the mice knew that.

I remember you,

the woman replied, wiping her painted eyes

with a scrap of lace so delicate

it looked like snowflakes sewn together.

You cured my sister and I,

when my father brought us here.

Dame Gothel inclined her head,

as if she was the princess,

as if she was the one wearing silk and velvet

and a white fur collar

instead of a grey dress

with badly embroidered ribbons

around the neck.

I knew they were badly embroidered,

I'd made them myself

for her last birthday

and I was still clumsy with a needle.

My bluebirds looked too fat

Briar Rose

to fly.
The princess kissed they boy's forehead.
I could tell he was feverish,
even from a distance.
His eyes fluttered like moths
caught in a candle flame.
When the carriage pulled away,
Dame Gothel sent me to gather willow leaves
for tea
and thyme to mix with honey.
I held cold compresses to his brow
even when he struggled weakly.
Dame Gothel rubbed his feet
and put an iron dagger under his pillow
to cut the fever.
I'd never had a friend before
and I was determined he should live.
I watched him through the night,
until I knew the exact number of his eyelashes,
the soft uncallused skin of his hands
and the rasping noise he made
when he was thirsty.
His hair was dark, like an otter's pelt.
I thought it beautiful,

more beautiful than my own yellow hair,

the colour of rancid butter.

I started to wash it with cold chamomile tea

and brushed all the burrs out.

After three long days

and three long nights,

he opened his eyes.

> *I've never met a prince before,*

I said.

He smiled shyly.

> *I thought you were a dream, a wild forest*
> *princess come to cure me.*

He lay back down wearily.

> *But princesses have long hair.*

That was the day I decided to grow my hair.

(iii)

After three more days

Dame Gothel pronounced him well enough

to walk outside.

She prescribed sunlight

and the sound of the river falling

over the rocks

Briar Rose

for all manner of illness.

I took him to my favourite place,

under the willow tree

whose leaves we'd brewed into tea

to fight his fever.

I tied a ribbon on a branch

to say thank you,

because wild forest girls

are polite that way.

I showed him my treasures:

a white pebble, the shells my father sent me

and a hawk feather.

He taught me to wield an invisible sword

and I taught him how to climb

the tallest tree.

Even when he was better,

I could climb the highest.

It never occurred to me not to.

He always looked down,

no matter how much I taunted him,

and tossed acorns at him like a squirrel.

He must have thought me feral,

but he never made me feel

as though I was any different from the other

Briar Rose

girls he knew,

though I was the dandelion

to their hothouse rose.

I only cared that we could run

through the forest

all day,

gathering berries

and fish for our supper.

    I wish I could stay here forever

he whispered one day

when we lay in the grass and counted fireflies.

(iv)

Too soon, Dame Gothel

pronounced him well enough

to go home

and the fine carriage

took him away

from me

and the willow tree

and the garden

where the rampion

used to

grow.

Briar Rose

Third Part...

(i)

I didn't see him again

for nearly three years.

I thought about him often

as my hair grew

down to my knees,

even though I hated

the time it took to brush the tangles out.

I still preferred the willow tree

to the village.

Dame Gothel's hands began to tremble

and she tired easily,

hunching over until she made a half moon crescent

of her body,

always bent over as if she was

searching for weeds in her garden.

She taught me how to sew wounds

together with tiny silk stitches

and coat them with honey and

cobwebs,

how to sing the old songs

Briar Rose

when brewing certain medicines

and when to answer

a

knock

at

the

back

door.

Every night I swore

I'd cut my hair,

and every night she smiled sadly

and knew I would not do it.

(ii)

She was the one who told me

there was power in hair.

She warned me to unbraid

the hair of a woman in labour,

or she'll stay stuck there forever,

and she taught me

that to wash with rosewater

and wrap red silk thread

through your hair

will bring

men to your door.

Fourth Part...

(i)

I was perched at the top of an oak tree

when I saw him next.

I'd been gathering pine resin for incense

and oak leaves for charms

when a horse bolted by,

hooves shaking the ground

so that even the branches trembled.

Moments later,

a muffled curse, and then a young man

with hair like

an otter's pelt

waking under my tree.

I tossed acorns at him again,

only this time it was an accident.

I was so startled to see him again,

I nearly lost my footing

and tumbled out of the tree altogether.

He drew his sword and glanced up,

those same beautiful eyes narrowed suspiciously.

I walked down the branches

as though they were marble steps,

pausing just out of reach.
When he recognized me, he smiled
and I swore the air
turned to honey.

I never thought I'd see you again,
he murmured.
I tilted my head, the way birds do
when they are waiting for what comes next.

Are you coming or not?
He laughed and tossed his sword aside
and pulled himself up
into the secret green embrace
of the forest.
He stopped, glancing down.
I leaned over and tickled him
with the end of my braid.

You still stop too soon.
He reached up and wound my hair
around his wrist
and tugged gently.

Rapunzel, Rapunzel
Let down your hair.
I wrapped it around a branch
and let him use it like a rope

to steady himself for the next step.
> *Only because you still can't climb*
> *a tree properly.*

He laughed when another man
might have shown anger.
> *You're not supposed to say things like that*
> *to a prince.*

I dropped down to the next branch, closer to him.
> *I'm not supposed to tell the truth? Anyway*
> *you used to tell me you wanted to be a*
> *woodcutter.*

He touched my hand, the gold ring
on his finger flashing.
I've missed you.
He sounded surprised.

(ii)
We followed the tracks of his horse,
back to Dame Gothel's cottage.
He wore a leather tunic etched with gold designs
and I wore a dress stained with berry juice
and leaves in my hair.
His boots cost more than my parents
abandoned house.

Briar Rose

I was barefoot.

His white horse was eating the grass

along the wall,

as Dame Gothel looped his reins

around an apple tree.

> *Dame Gothel, you saved my life*
> *all those years ago.*

The prince kissed the back of her hand

as if she was a queen

and I loved him

a little more.

We fed him honey on thick brown bread,

apples and rosehip tea.

He told us stories of jousting,

of men who juggled fire and knives

at knightly tournaments in countries

where the deserts stretched all the way to the sky.

I told him about the turtle eggs by the river,

and the way the northern lights

dance

when

it

is

cold

outside.
Dame Gothel fell asleep
in her chair.

(iii)
She never woke up.

(iv)
The rain was cold at the windows
for the next three days,
and the dogs would not be consoled.
On the third morning,
a carriage pulled up to the cottage
with a royal invitation.
I went because I missed him,
even though I preferred the smoky cottage
to a thousand fire jugglers and feather beds,
just as Dame Gothel had.
I went because
one does not refuse a royal invitation.
The dogs stayed with the baker.
I didn't envy them at the time.

Fifth Part...

(i)

I was given my own rooms

with tapestries and a window seat

where I could see the knights

on the practice field,

and the girls who pretended

not to watch them.

Their hair was long and pretty

and plaited with jewels,

but mine,

I noticed,

was the longest.

One of the poets wrote

about it

and

that night I held the flat of my knife

to my braid.

But still I did not cut.

(ii)

I learned to dance

and curtsy

and which fork to use at supper.

None of that mattered,

only the late nights

whispering in the window seat

with the prince.

In the afternoons, he was formal

and wore velvet and

bowed to all the girls.

At night, we talked about

how he hated to dance

and

how at least

if he was chopping firewood

he would be doing something useful.

He especially hated the poem about my hair.

(iii)

There were no trees to climb

on the castle grounds.

The orchards were full

of fruit trees trained to grow wide

and easy to pick.

I didn't know why that made me want to cry.

Briar Rose

(iv)

I found solace in the gardens,

pulling weeds and

gathering flowers for tonics.

The girls came to my door at midnight

asking for love potions.

At dawn,

the boys did the same.

I made a tincture for the old king's gout

and tea for his wife's nerves.

When one of the scullery maids

dropped a knife on her foot,

I stitched up the wound

and treated it with honey and spider webs,

just as Dame Gothel taught me,

and I missed her

fiercely.

I longed for the trees

and the cottage

and the

back door.

I longed for it

the way my mother

had longed for

rampion.

(v)

When it rained

the prince and I hid

in the cellar

with the wine barrels

and kissed

and

my

hair

grew

longer

and

longer.

(vi)

His mother invited me to her parlour

where everything

was painted with gold

and it hurt my eyes to look on it.

Seven ladies-in-waiting fluttered

around her like butterflies
until she waved them off.
I remembered actual butterflies
and the way they hovered
around the milkweed,
which was good for gallstones
and poison.
But it was just her and me
and all that gold,
making her look jaundiced.
> *Proper ladies don't meddle*
> *in medicine and other such*
> *messy business.*

I didn't know what to say
but luckily I was only required to be
silent.
Dame Gothel was a gifted healer
> *And I'll always honour her memory*
> *for saving my son,*
> *but she didn't live at court*
> *and princes don't marry*
> *orphans*
> *who treat scullery maids*
> *and lance warts.*

Briar Rose

They whisper you're a witch
and that will not do.
You know what they say about witches.

(vii)

There are traditions,
the prince said to me that night
when he found me
hiding in the pear orchard.
You can still make your teas
and tinctures,
only do it secretly.
I shredded leaves between my fingers.
And if I asked you only to be a prince
in private,
could you?
He kissed me then.
I am already only myself in private,
with you.
I pulled away,
and knew by the look on his face,
that I was the first girl
to ever pull away.
And that's enough for you?

He shrugged.

> *I was born a prince, it's no use still wishing*
> *I was a woodcutter.*

I shook my head and longed for the smoky

air of the cottage.

> *But I wasn't born a princess.*

(viii)

That night I cut off all of my hair.

Sixth Part...

(i)

I left the next morning.

I walked for the whole day,

until my dainty silk slippers wore through

and I was barefoot again,

feeling the grass and the mud

and the acorns

between my toes.

He didn't come after me.

The dogs had abandoned the baker

and were waiting for me

Briar Rose

at the back door,

knowing in the way

that

dogs know.

(ii)

I swept the floor

and sorted through the

glass bottles

of tonics and seeds

and pretended that I wasn't listening

for the sound of a carriage,

a horse,

anything.

(iii)

The first knock

came at midnight

and it helped,

even though

it was only the baker's daughter

who had eaten too many

Briar Rose

mince meat pies again.

The next morning,

I climbed the oak tree and it helped too,

but I still glanced at the road

every time a twig snapped.

I heard stories about the prince

and how sad he looked

and that kings sent their

daughters

from all over the world

to cheer him up.

(iv)

The next knock came at midnight

at the back door.

He was on his knees,

not begging,

but bleeding.

His fine tunic was torn,

his arms muddy

and his beautiful face

streaked with sweat and

blood.

He blinked as if he couldn't see me,

even with the lantern light on my face.

    Rapunzel, Rapunzel

    Let down your hair.

I crouched down

as he reached with broken fingers

for my hair.

    I cut it

I said before he could touch me.

    Good

he replied as I put my arm under his shoulders

to help him inside,

    You always hated it.

I never realized he had noticed.

(v)

He told me he had climbed the highest tree he could

find

just to see the roof of my cottage.

    You never could climb,

I replied, mixing ointment for his eyes.

    I fell into a patch of thorns

he admitted,

as I pulled one of those thorns

from his eyebrow.

You have healers at the castle,

I said.

Yes

he replied even as his cuts began to bleed again

But you are here.

I wrapped his eyes with a clean cloth

dipped in meadowsweet water

and sang a song Dame Gothel used

to sing to me,

and wished I could knock

at her back door

for advice.

But there was only me, the dogs

and a blind prince.

(vi)

The next day

he still could not see,

though he touched my face,

my neck

and my hair

with his fingertips.

I'm sorry I waited so long

he said softly

Briar Rose

> *But some of us aren't as brave*
> *as you are.*

(vii)
The second day
he asked if he could stay
and I didn't know how to answer
except to say
> *I can't be your princess.*

He reached for my hands
which were already callused
from my work tending to the
neglected gardens.
> *But I can be your woodcutter.*
> *Besides, I never did like poetry*
> *or swords.*

And then he kissed me
until I cried
and when my tears
touched his lashes,
the last of the blood washed away
and he could see again.
I had short hair,
grass stains on my hem,

Briar Rose

and dirt under my fingernails.
It was midnight,
and I was
at the back door
of the witch's cottage,
wanting love
as much as the villagers
who knocked
in the night.

(viii)
On the third day,
while I was up in the willow tree
gathering bark for headache tea,
the carriage came back.
It was as perfect as ever,
as if it was made of marzipan.
I ran as fast as I could,
heedless of the stones
cutting into my feet,
and the pine boughs scratching my face.
I only heard the creak
of carriage wheels
echoing like thunder

Briar Rose

and horse hooves like hail on

the roof of the cottage

the prince

had claimed to want to see so badly.

(ix)

I was too late.

(x)

I watched the carriage rumble away

until I felt as if I was being crushed,

like seeds in a mortar.

(xi)

When he stepped out of the shadows,

I thought him one of spirits

Dame Gothel used to warn me about.

But it was only the prince

in his torn tunic stained with blood

and his eyes

watching me

watching him.

    They came looking for a prince,

he said

Briar Rose

>*but there was only a woodcutter.*

He slipped his hand in mine

and there was no talk of rings

or wedding vows,

only love.

(xii)

And a warning:

>*They will come back,*

I smiled and led him

to the back door

and said

>*If they come back*
>*they will find a woodcutter*
>*and a witch,*
>*and you know what they say*
>*about witches.*

xiii)

Somewhere on the castle grounds,

belladonna

blooms.

Briar Rose

Part 6

The Witch

Briar Rose

Briar Rose

The Witch

I have never cared for sweets

and I have certainly never

lived in a house made of

sugar

and gingerbread.

Never mind that icing

won't keep the cold out,

I could never have afforded

the price of sugar,

and ginger makes me

sneeze.

***

I lived alone

with the cardinals

and the butterfly cocoons

dangling like pale green lanterns

from the trees.

I was careful

to keep the axe sharp

and the

poppy seeds

from the

pepper.

I was careful

to keep the candles

from the curtains

and the goat

from the lettuce patch.

I was careful to leave cream out

for the Good Neighbours

and to pour honey mead

over the roots of the

oak tree

when thunder shook the sky.

***

I was not careful enough.

***

The village folk

assumed I was creating the

lightning

when I was only being

polite,

as my mother taught me.

***

When the young ones

followed a trail of white pebbles

back home

and were locked out,

why do you still look my way?

Surely the father

who closed his eyes

and ears

is to blame,

and the mother

who let the hunger in her belly

grow bigger than the

babes who'd once

lived there.

Briar Rose

***

Perhaps it doesn't read as well
that I am not the villain
simply for being old and wise
and a woman,
and you would prefer me with the
blood of children
on my chin,
but that says more about
you
then it does about
me.

About the Author

Alyxandra Harvey lives in an old Victorian stone house with her husband, dogs, and a few friendly ghosts. She loves medieval dresses, used to be able to recite all of The Lady of Shalott by Tennyson, and has been accused, more than once, of being born in the wrong century. She believes this to be mostly true, except for the fact that she really likes running water, women's rights, and ice cream.
She likes cinnamon lattes, tattoos and books.

She is the author of the Drake Chronicles, Haunting Violet and Stolen Away.

Visit her at: www.alyxandraharvey.com

Briar Rose

Manor House Publishing